Brave Baby Elephant

BRAVE
BABY
ELEPHANT

by Sesyle Joslin

pictures by Leonard Weisgard

11198

HARCOURT, BRACE AND COMPANY, NEW YORK

E

4 - 14 - 6 1

For Tory, Andy, Julie,

Stephie, and Burnes

with love

Baby Elephant and his mother were in the kitchen.
Baby Elephant sat at the table eating his supper.

"I am thinking," Baby Elephant said, "that perhaps I should remind you."

"Of what?" asked Mother Elephant.

"Of tonight is the night of my adventure. I am going by myself. All alone."

"Oh, yes, I know. I wouldn't forget such a thing."

"I didn't really think you would."

Baby Elephant finished his supper.

"Mother Elephant," he said, "because it is night and I am going by myself, I think I should have some more to eat. Don't you agree?"

"Oh, yes, I quite agree," said Mother Elephant, and she gave Baby Elephant more mashed potatoes, more string beans, and another loaf of bread, all of which he ate up quickly, as baby elephants will.

"Mother Elephant, I am sitting here and wondering."

"Yes, I can see that you are."

"I am wondering if perhaps I may please have some dessert?" said Baby Elephant, who was a polite baby elephant generally but most particularly when desserts were concerned.

"You may," said his mother, "and because this is the first time you are going to go by yourself, all alone, I have made you a special dessert called The Baby Elephant Dessert."

"Aha," said Baby Elephant greedily, "I am glad to hear that. If it is called The Baby Elephant Dessert, it must be quite large."

Mother Elephant snorted and trumpeted and shook all over with laughter.

"My silly baby elephant," she said. "I named the dessert The Baby Elephant Dessert because it is *for* you, not because it is large and gray with big ears and a long trunk."

Mother Elephant went to the cupboard and took out a cake covered with pink and white icing and decorated with cherries.

"Here is The Baby Elephant Dessert. Although, as you can see, it does not look like you."

"No," said Baby Elephant. "It does not look like
me at all. It is prettier."

"Well," said Mother Elephant, "perhaps just a
little."

"But it is delicious, all the same," said Baby
Elephant.

"I am glad to hear that," said Mother Elephant.
Baby Elephant ate up all his cake.

"Mother Elephant?"

"Yes?"

"I am thinking that now it is time for me to get all the things I will need to take along on my adventure. Don't you agree?"

"Oh, yes, I quite agree."

"And then I shall come back to kiss you before I go," said Baby Elephant.

"I am glad to hear that," said Mother Elephant.

Baby Elephant went to the hall closet.

"To begin with," he said, "I shall wear this fur coat that Uncle Elephant left here last month. It will keep me nice and warm.

"And I shall wear Grandfather Elephant's top hat. It is splendid-looking, and if I meet anyone, they are sure to say, 'My, what an elegant and grown-up Baby Elephant *he* is!'"

Baby Elephant looked into the closet again.

"And naturally I shall wear Father Elephant's handsome boots because it is a fierce winter's night."

Baby Elephant, dressed in Uncle Elephant's fur coat, Grandfather Elephant's top hat, and Father Elephant's boots, went into his playroom.

"To begin with," he said, "I know I shall need my lantern.

"And I had better take my sword. Just in case.

"And, of course, I will take Bear because.

"Now," Baby Elephant asked himself, "is there anything else I shall need when I am by myself all alone?"

Baby Elephant thought very hard, and then he answered himself.

"Of course, you silly baby elephant, there is something else. There is food."

Baby Elephant, dressed in Uncle Elephant's fur coat, Grandfather Elephant's top hat, and Father Elephant's boots, and carrying his lantern, his sword, and Bear, went back to the kitchen.

"Mother Elephant?"

"Is that you, Baby Elephant?"

"Yes," said Baby Elephant.

"I just wondered," said Mother Elephant.

"I believe I need some food, Mother Elephant."

Mother Elephant flapped her ears. "*What?*" she
said. "But you have only just had supper, two help-
ings of everything, and a whole pink and white cake
with cherries, as well."

Baby Elephant nodded his head. "That is all per-
fectly true," he said, "but I am thinking of later. I

am thinking that I might get hungry after I leave you. Don't you think that is possible?"

"I am thinking perhaps anything is possible with a baby elephant," Mother Elephant said. "Here is a Thermos of milk and here is a napkin full of cookies, and I shall put them in this basket for you."

"Thank you, Mother Elephant."

"You are very welcome."

"You are a good mother elephant," Baby Elephant said.

"I try," said Mother Elephant.

Baby Elephant and his mother went into the living room, where Grandmother Elephant and Grandfather Elephant and Father Elephant were sitting around the fire.

Baby Elephant went up to his grandmother.

"Pip, pip, Grandmother Elephant," he said. "I am on my way," and because that did not seem quite enough to say, he added, "I hope you will be feeling fine while I am gone."

"Thank you, Baby Elephant," Grandmother Elephant said. "I am sure I will be feeling fine. But let me have a good look at you. My, what an elegant and grown-up baby elephant you are!"

Baby Elephant was very pleased.

"Ho," he said. "Do you know, I just thought somebody might say that very thing."

Baby Elephant approached his grandfather.

"Here I go, sir," he said.

"Harrrumph," said Grandfather Elephant. "That is a familiar-looking top hat you are wearing. Very splendid."

"I am glad you like it, sir," said Baby Elephant.

"Ah, me!" Grandmother Elephant sighed. "I can scarcely believe that Baby Elephant is big enough to go by himself. Why, I can remember when he was a very tiny baby elephant. And what is more, I can remember when his mother was a very tiny baby elephant."

"Harrrumph," said Grandfather Elephant. "What's so extraordinary about that, eh? I wouldn't think I was much of an elephant if I couldn't remember further back than that. Why, I can remember when everybody was a very tiny baby elephant, and you, my dear," he said gallantly to Grandmother Elephant, "you were the tiniest of them all."

Grandmother Elephant snorted happily. "Tish-tosh!" she said.

Baby Elephant approached his father.

"Well, Father Elephant," he said, "I am on my way, and I hope, sir, to make you proud."

"I hope the very same thing," said Father Elephant.

"Remember that I shall be here if you ever need me. By the way, Baby Elephant, those are familiar-looking boots you are wearing. Very handsome."

"I am glad you like them, sir," said Baby Elephant.

Baby Elephant kissed his mother.

"You will know if I arrive safely because I shall find a way to send you a message. Meanwhile, I hope you will not worry about me too much."

"I will try not to, Baby Elephant."

Baby Elephant started to leave.

"Baby Elephant?"

"Yes, Mother Elephant?"

"You haven't forgotten your teeth, have you?"

Baby Elephant put down his lantern, his sword, Bear, and his basket of food, and reached way into his mouth.

"No, Mother Elephant," he said. "I haven't forgotten my teeth. They are still there."

Mother Elephant snorted and trumpeted and shook all over with laughter.

"My silly baby elephant," she said. "I mean you haven't forgotten *about* them. About brushing them."

"Oh," said Baby Elephant. "I shall go and brush them right now, this very minute, because who knows when I shall get another chance?"

Baby Elephant, dressed in Uncle Elephant's fur coat, Grandfather Elephant's top hat, and Father Elephant's boots, and carrying his lantern, his sword, Bear, and his basket of food, went upstairs.

Baby Elephant brushed his teeth very carefully, and he washed his face, as well.

Baby Elephant looked into the mirror and said, "That is an extraordinary, clean and brave baby elephant, if I do say so myself."

Baby Elephant left the bathroom.

"Well," he said. "Here I go, by myself. All alone."
And holding his lantern up and his sword out, Baby
Elephant walked bravely down the long hall. He
turned bravely into his bedroom and jumped bravely
into his bed, pulling the covers well over his head.

"I have done it!" Baby Elephant said. "I have cer-
tainly done it. All alone and by myself."

Baby Elephant slowly poked his trunk out from under the covers, and then his head. He took off Grandfather Elephant's top hat and put it on the bedpost. He put his lantern on the bedside table, and he placed his sword under his pillow. He put Bear on guard at the foot of the bed, and then he drank his milk and ate his cookies.

"And now," said Baby Elephant, "I must get word to Mother Elephant and Father Elephant and Grandmother Elephant and Grandfather Elephant that I have arrived safely."

Baby Elephant stood up in his bed
and trumpeted loudly:

"GOOD NIGHT, EVERYBODY!"

And everybody trumpeted back:

"GOOD NIGHT, BABY ELEPHANT!"